Britta Teckentrup

Oskar

loves...

Prestel
Munich · London · New York

This is Oskar.

Oskar loves the deep blue ocean...

...and soft green grass.

Oskar loves the smell of spring...

...and yellow autumn leaves.

Oskar loves sweet red cherries...

...and his favourite pebble.

Oskar loves to watch the world from above...

...and take his little fluffy cloud for a walk.

Oskar loves to lose himself in books…

...and pictures.

Oskar loves the rain…

...and the sun.

Oskar loves walking in the moonlight…

...and the silence of snow.

What do you love?

© 2016, Prestel Verlag, Munich · London · New York
A member of Verlagsgruppe Random House GmbH
Neumarkter Strasse 28 · 81673 Munich

Prestel Publishing Ltd.
14-17 Wells Street
London W1T 3PD

Prestel Publishing
900 Broadway, Suite 603
New York, NY 10003

Library of Congress Control Number: 2016936146.
A CIP catalogue record for this book is available
from the British Library.

Editorial direction: Doris Kutschbach
Production management: Astrid Wedemeyer
Typesetting: textum GmbH
Printing and binding: TBB, a.s. Banská Bystrica
Paper: Tauro

Verlagsgruppe Random House FSC® N001967

Printed in Slovakia

ISBN 978-3-7913-7270-9
www.prestel.com

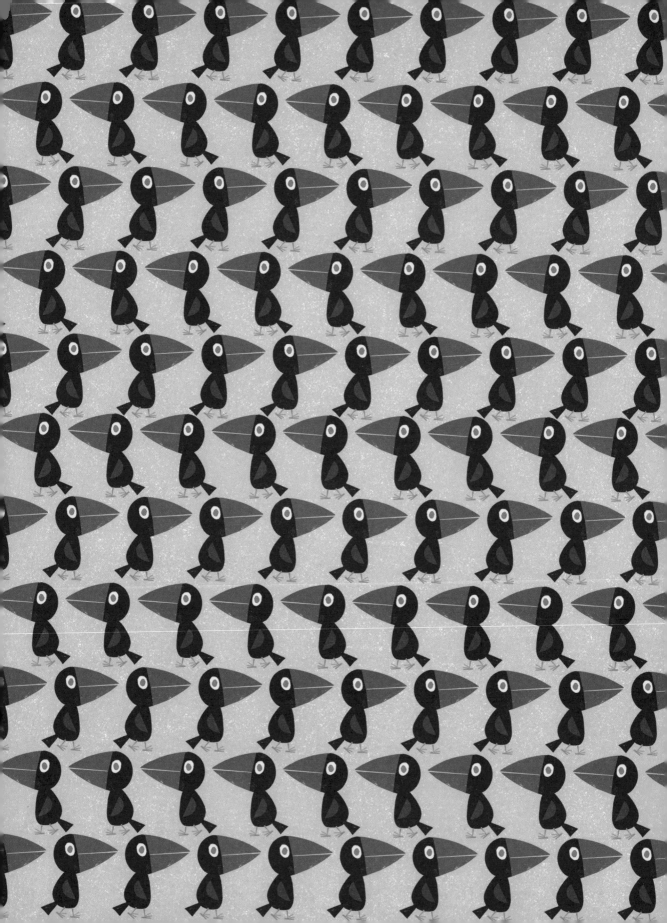